™

This book is dedicated to all of my family.
Thank you for always supporting me!

~Danny Moore

RAYMOND'S

GAMEDAY ADVENTURE

Written & Illustrated By Danny Moore

It was a beautiful morning in the Sunshine State. Raymond, the beloved mascot of the Tampa Bay Rays, was just waking up and getting ready to face the day.

He had a lot to do, so he knew he needed to get dressed fast.
The mascot didn't have a single moment to spare!

Raymond climbed into the Rays Hummer and made the short drive up I-4 to Orlando, the theme park capital of the world!

There was so much to do there, Raymond didn't know where to start! He rushed from park to park, taking his turn riding the roller coasters, watching some of the spectacular shows, and greeting all of the fellow Rays fans from around the globe.

After finishing up his escapades in Orlando, Raymond headed back towards St. Petersburg. Along the way, he traveled through downtown Tampa. He marveled at the skyline and some of the sensational architecture that makes Tampa such a unique city. Rays fans saw him driving by and yelled, "Hey, Raymond! Go Rays!"

While he was in the city, he hopped on the trolley that runs through Channelside down to Ybor City, checking out historic sites along the way.

From Ybor City, the mascot scooted down to the water and leapt into a speedboat with some fellow Rays fans. They sped off together across the bay. It was a bumpy ride, but Raymond loved feeling the wind through his hair.

The captain slowed the boat down and prepared the crew for some sport fishing. Raymond grabbed a fishing pole and tossed out a line behind the boat. It wasn't long before a great big marlin took the bait! The mighty brute put up a tremendous fight, but the mascot managed to reel in the monster fish. He posed for a quick photo, and everyone patted Raymond on the back. "Nice catch!" they all shouted.

Without a moment to spare, the captain started the motor
and they took off towards the stadium. Raymond was amazed
by the size and design of the Sunshine Skyway as the boat
zipped along beside it. He was happy to know that it was
considered the "flag bridge" of Florida.

After all that fun in the sun, it was time to get
ready for some baseball. The mascot made his way
towards the Trop. He could feel the excitement in
the air, for today was Raymond Bobblehead Day!
All of the youngest Rays fans received their very
own mini-version of Raymond. The mascot loved
seeing all of the fans dressed in blue and gold with
cowbells in hand. He gave everyone high fives
along his way until his palms were sore.

Raymond walked down to the field to check out some of the pre-game action. Today was a special day because some of the younger Rays fans got a chance to play catch with their favorite Rays players on the field before the game. Raymond grabbed a glove and joined in on the fun.

Next, it was time for batting practice. The mascot
watched as each Ray took his turn warming up.
Some swung for the fences and a few of them
knocked the ball clean out of the park. The players
yelled, "Hey, Raymond! Did you see that?"

The game was about to start, so everyone took their seats. The players were introduced and ran onto the field along with their Baseball Buddy—a local little leaguer from the Tampa Bay area. They all took their places along the first base line.

The stadium grew silent for the national anthem. A young girl sang out a beautiful rendition of the song, causing the crowd to cheer very loudly when she was finished. Raymond ran up to the mound and tossed out the ceremonial first pitch. He felt so proud to be a part of the Tampa Bay Rays family.

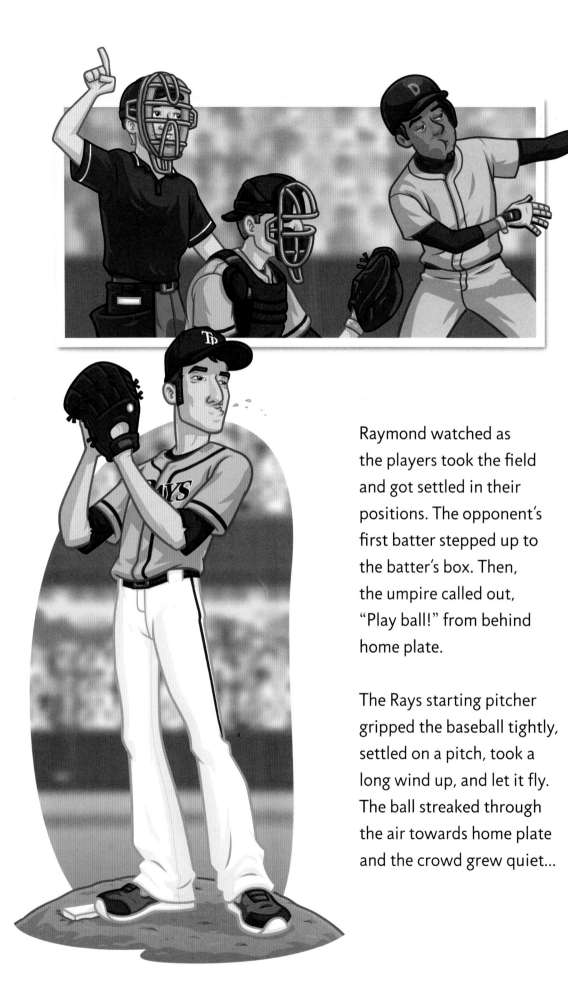

Raymond watched as the players took the field and got settled in their positions. The opponent's first batter stepped up to the batter's box. Then, the umpire called out, "Play ball!" from behind home plate.

The Rays starting pitcher gripped the baseball tightly, settled on a pitch, took a long wind up, and let it fly. The ball streaked through the air towards home plate and the crowd grew quiet...

"Steeeeeeeee-rike, one!" yelled the ump. Everyone cheered. Raymond knew that this was going to be a great game and couldn't wait to see what was going to happen next.

As the game progressed, the Rays played some
spectacular baseball. Raymond mingled through the
crowd and entertained the fans with his crazy high jinks.
Everyone screamed, "Raymond, you're so funny!"

All that running around made the mascot very
hungry, so he made his way to the concessions area.
He couldn't wait to get his hands on a famous Rays
Cuban sandwich.

Raymond strolled over to the Rays Touch Tank as he ate to visit some of his ray pals. They looked as hungry as he had been earlier, so he fed them some delicious fish snacks.

With a belly full of food, Raymond had to take a break. He sat and watched some of the excitement on the field. He was amazed by the speed of the players as they stole the bases and the power behind their bats.

He loved seeing the fantastic defensive plays at third base and short stop and watching the sliding catch made out in center field. They all did their parts in a fantastic display of brilliant baseball.

It was finally the ninth inning and the Rays had a five to nothing lead. So far, not a single player on the opposing team had gotten a hit off of the fire from the Rays pitcher. It all came down to the last batter, with one out left in the game.

The crowd all held their breath as the last fastball was hurled towards home plate. The hitter swung hard and cracked a pop-fly into right field.

The right fielder was there waiting. The player launched himself into a backwards dive and stuck out his glove. He reached out as far as his arm would go and snagged the ball out of the air. The fans went wild! The pitcher had thrown a no-hitter!

The whole team gathered at the pitcher's mound and celebrated hysterically. Raymond joined the party on the field as they all jumped up and down together. It was a wonderful moment in baseball history.

After all that celebrating and such a long, exhilarating day, Raymond was very tired. As he made his way home, all the fans cheered, "Go Rays! Go Rays!" The mascot knew he was going to have an excellent night's sleep.

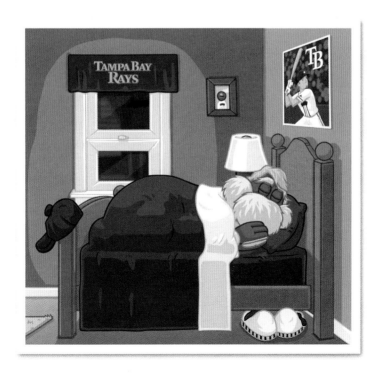

The Tampa Bay Rays logo above appears in this
book a total of 15 times. See if you can go back and
find them all! Some are a little tougher to find than
others, so look closely. The logo above counts
as number 1. Now only 14 more to go!

www.mascotbooks.com

For more information, please contact:
Mascot Books
P.O. Box 220157
Chantilly, VA 20153-0157
info@mascotbooks.com

ISBN: 1-936319-01-2
ISBN-13: 978-1-936319-01-5
CPSIA Code: PRT0111A

Printed in the United States

Check out some of our many titles!

Baseball

Boston Red Sox	*Hello, Wally!*	Jerry Remy
Boston Red Sox	*Wally The Green Monster And His Journey Through Red Sox Nation!*	Jerry Remy
Boston Red Sox	*Coast to Coast with Wally The Green Monster*	Jerry Remy
Boston Red Sox	*A Season with Wally The Green Monster*	Jerry Remy
Colorado Rockies	*Hello, Dinger!*	Aimee Aryal
Detroit Tigers	*Hello, Paws!*	Aimee Aryal
New York Yankees	*Let's Go, Yankees!*	Yogi Berra
New York Yankees	*Yankees Town*	Aimee Aryal
New York Mets	*Hello, Mr. Met!*	Rusty Staub
New York Mets	*Mr. Met and his Journey Through the Big Apple*	Aimee Aryal
St. Louis Cardinals	*Hello, Fredbird!*	Ozzie Smith
Philadelphia Phillies	*Hello, Phillie Phanatic!*	Aimee Aryal
Chicago Cubs	*Let's Go, Cubs!*	Aimee Aryal
Chicago White Sox	*Let's Go, White Sox!*	Aimee Aryal
Cleveland Indians	*Hello, Slider!*	Bob Feller
Seattle Mariners	*Hello, Mariner Moose!*	Aimee Aryal
Washington Nationals	*Hello, Screech!*	Aimee Aryal
Milwaukee Brewers	*Hello, Bernie Brewer!*	Aimee Aryal

College

Alabama	*Hello, Big Al!*	Aimee Aryal
Alabama	*Roll Tide!*	Ken Stabler
Alabama	*Big Al's Journey Through the Yellowhammer State*	Aimee Aryal
Arizona	*Hello, Wilbur!*	Lute Olson
Arizona State	*Hello, Sparky!*	Aimee Aryal
Arkansas	*Hello, Big Red!*	Aimee Aryal
Arkansas	*Big Red's Journey Through the Razorback State*	Aimee Aryal
Auburn	*Hello, Aubie!*	Aimee Aryal
Auburn	*War Eagle!*	Pat Dye
Auburn	*Aubie's Journey Through the Yellowhammer State*	Aimee Aryal
Boston College	*Hello, Baldwin!*	Aimee Aryal
Brigham Young	*Hello, Cosmo!*	LaVell Edwards
Cal - Berkeley	*Hello, Oski!*	Aimee Aryal
Clemson	*Hello, Tiger!*	Aimee Aryal
Clemson	*Tiger's Journey Through the Palmetto State*	Aimee Aryal
Colorado	*Hello, Ralphie!*	Aimee Aryal
Connecticut	*Hello, Jonathan!*	Aimee Aryal
Duke	*Hello, Blue Devil!*	Aimee Aryal
Florida	*Hello, Albert!*	Aimee Aryal
Florida	*Albert's Journey Through the Sunshine State*	Aimee Aryal
Florida State	*Let's Go, 'Noles!*	Aimee Aryal
Georgia	*Hello, Hairy Dawg!*	Aimee Aryal
Georgia	*How 'Bout Them Dawgs!*	Vince Dooley
Georgia	*Hairy Dawg's Journey Through the Peach State*	Vince Dooley
Georgia Tech	*Hello, Buzz!*	Aimee Aryal
Gonzaga	*Spike, The Gonzaga Bulldog*	Mike Pringle
Illinois	*Let's Go, Illini!*	Aimee Aryal
Indiana	*Let's Go, Hoosiers!*	Aimee Aryal
Iowa	*Hello, Herky!*	Aimee Aryal
Iowa State	*Hello, Cy!*	Amy DeLashmutt
James Madison	*Hello, Duke Dog!*	Aimee Aryal
Kansas	*Hello, Big Jay!*	Aimee Aryal
Kansas State	*Hello, Willie!*	Dan Walter
Kentucky	*Hello, Wildcat!*	Aimee Aryal
LSU	*Hello, Mike!*	Aimee Aryal
LSU	*Mike's Journey Through the Bayou State*	Aimee Aryal
Maryland	*Hello, Testudo!*	Aimee Aryal
Michigan	*Let's Go, Blue!*	Aimee Aryal
Michigan State	*Hello, Sparty!*	Aimee Aryal
Michigan State	*Sparty's Journey Through Michigan*	Aimee Aryal
Middle Tennessee	*Hello, Lightning!*	Aimee Aryal
Minnesota	*Hello, Goldy!*	Aimee Aryal
Mississippi	*Hello, Colonel Rebel!*	Aimee Aryal

Pro Football

Carolina Panthers	*Let's Go, Panthers!*	Aimee Aryal
Chicago Bears	*Let's Go, Bears!*	Aimee Aryal
Dallas Cowboys	*How 'Bout Them Cowboys!*	Aimee Aryal
Green Bay Packers	*Go, Pack, Go!*	Aimee Aryal
Kansas City Chiefs	*Let's Go, Chiefs!*	Aimee Aryal
Minnesota Vikings	*Let's Go, Vikings!*	Aimee Aryal
New York Giants	*Let's Go, Giants!*	Aimee Aryal
New York Jets	*J-E-T-S! Jets, Jets, Jets!*	Aimee Aryal
New England Patriots	*Let's Go, Patriots!*	Aimee Aryal
Pittsburg Steelers	*Here We Go, Steelers!*	Aimee Aryal
Seattle Seahawks	*Let's Go, Seahawks!*	Aimee Aryal
Washington Redskins	*Hail To The Redskins!*	Aimee Aryal

Basketball

Dallas Mavericks	*Let's Go, Mavs!*	Mark Cuban
Boston Celtics	*Let's Go, Celtics!*	Aimee Aryal

Other

Kentucky Derby	*White Diamond Runs For The Roses*	Aimee Aryal
Marine Corps Marathon	*Run, Miles, Run!*	Aimee Aryal

Mississippi State	*Hello, Bully!*	Aimee Aryal
Missouri	*Hello, Truman!*	Todd Donoho
Missouri	*Hello, Truman! Show Me Missouri!*	Todd Donoho
Nebraska	*Hello, Herbie Husker!*	Aimee Aryal
North Carolina	*Hello, Rameses!*	Aimee Aryal
North Carolina	*Rameses' Journey Through the Tar Heel State*	Aimee Aryal
North Carolina St.	*Hello, Mr. Wuf!*	Aimee Aryal
North Carolina St.	*Mr. Wuf's Journey Through North Carolina*	Aimee Aryal
Northern Arizona	*Hello, Louie!*	Jeanette S. Baker
Notre Dame	*Let's Go, Irish!*	Aimee Aryal
Ohio State	*Hello, Brutus!*	Aimee Aryal
Ohio State	*Brutus' Journey*	Aimee Aryal
Oklahoma	*Let's Go, Sooners!*	Aimee Aryal
Oklahoma State	*Hello, Pistol Pete!*	Aimee Aryal
Oregon	*Go Ducks!*	Aimee Aryal
Oregon State	*Hello, Benny the Beaver!*	Aimee Aryal
Penn State	*Hello, Nittany Lion!*	Aimee Aryal
Penn State	*We Are Penn State!*	Joe Paterno
Purdue	*Hello, Purdue Pete!*	Aimee Aryal
Rutgers	*Hello, Scarlet Knight!*	Aimee Aryal
South Carolina	*Hello, Cocky!*	Aimee Aryal
South Carolina	*Cocky's Journey Through the Palmetto State*	Aimee Aryal
So. California	*Hello, Tommy Trojan!*	Aimee Aryal
Syracuse	*Hello, Otto!*	Aimee Aryal
Tennessee	*Hello, Smokey!*	Aimee Aryal
Tennessee	*Smokey's Journey Through the Volunteer State*	Aimee Aryal
Texas	*Hello, Hook 'Em!*	Aimee Aryal
Texas	*Hook 'Em's Journey Through the Lone Star State*	Aimee Aryal
Texas A & M	*Howdy, Reveille!*	Aimee Aryal
Texas A & M	*Reveille's Journey Through the Lone Star State*	Aimee Aryal
Texas Tech	*Hello, Masked Rider!*	Aimee Aryal
UCLA	*Hello, Joe Bruin!*	Aimee Aryal
Virginia	*Hello, CavMan!*	Aimee Aryal
Virginia Tech	*Hello, Hokie Bird!*	Aimee Aryal
Virginia Tech	*Yea, It's Hokie Game Day!*	Frank Beamer
Virginia Tech	*Hokie Bird's Journey Through Virginia*	Aimee Aryal
Wake Forest	*Hello, Demon Deacon!*	Aimee Aryal
Washington	*Hello, Harry the Husky!*	Aimee Aryal
Washington State	*Hello, Butch!*	Aimee Aryal
West Virginia	*Hello, Mountaineer!*	Aimee Aryal
West Virginia	*The Mountaineer's Journey Through West Virginia*	Leslie H. Haning
Wisconsin	*Hello, Bucky!*	Aimee Aryal
Wisconsin	*Bucky's Journey Through the Badger State*	Aimee Aryal

Order online at mascotbooks.com using promo code *free* to receive FREE SHIPPING!

More great titles coming soon!

SCHOOL PROGRAM

Promote reading. Build spirit. Raise money.™

Mascot Books® is creating customized children's books for public and private elementary schools all across America. Containing school-specific story lines and illustrations, our books are beloved by principals, librarians, teachers, parents, and of course, by young readers.

Our books feature your mascot taking a tour of your school, while highlighting all the things and events that make your school community such a special place.

The Mascot Books Elementary School Program is an innovative way to promote reading and build spirit, while offering a fresh, new marketing or fundraising opportunity.

Starting Is As Easy As 1-2-3!

1 You tell us all about your school community. What makes your school unique? What are your well-known traditions? Why do parents and students love your school?

2 With the information you share with us, Mascot Books creates a one-of-a-kind hardcover children's book featuring your school and your mascot.

3 Your book is delivered!

Great new fundraising idea for public schools!

Innovative way to market your private school to potential new students!

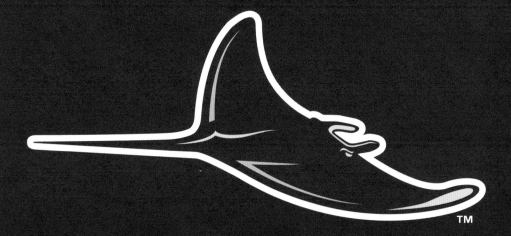

TB™